Miss Tutus Star

By Lesléa Newman

Illustrated by Carey Armstrong-Ellis

Abrams Books for Young Readers
New York

Selena was a little girl

Who did not walk so much as twirl,

Who did not skip so much as prance,

Because Selena loved to dance.

While all her friends ran off to play,
Selena practiced her ballet.

She danced until her feet were sore,
And then Selena danced some more.

Her mother knew just what to do.

"We're off to visit Miss Tutu."

The famous teacher let them in,
Clapped her hands, and said, "Begin."

Selena took some steps with flair
And landed on her derrière.
She sighed and said, "I'm such a klutz."
Miss Tutu said, "But you've got guts.

You've got passion, you've got style.
Grace will come after a while.
With hard work, you'll be a star.
Now put your foot upon the barre."

"Arabesque,

and pas de bourrée.

Pirouette,

and demi-plié.

Pas de chat,

and relevé.

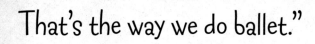

That's the way we do ballet."

Selena mixed up left and right.
Her grand jeté was quite a sight.
Still she always tried her best.
She made mistakes, but on she pressed.

"Shoulders down and stomach in,
As round and round the room you spin.
Feel the music, hear the beat,
And softly land upon your feet."

Even when Selena fell,
Miss Tutu said, "You're doing well.
What matters most is from the start,
My dear, you've always danced with heart."

Dressed in tights and leotard,
Selena studied very hard.

The years passed by, first one,

then two,

And then came time for her debut.
In satin shoes and pink tutu,
Selena waited for her cue.

"I can't go on!" Selena cried.
The truth is, she was terrified.

Miss Tutu touched Selena's arm.
"My dear, there's no need for alarm.
Just smile, relax, and take your stance,
Then show the world your love of dance."

The curtains parted with a squeak.
Miss Tutu kissed Selena's cheek.
Selena smiled and took her pose,
Then crossed the stage upon her toes.

She spun so fast and jumped so high,
Selena looked like she could fly.

And when her dancing was complete,
The audience leaped to its feet.

"Three cheers!" her fans cried out. "Bravo!
Selena, how we love you so!"
Selena looked about. "What now?"
Miss Tutu whispered, "Take your bow."

For Miranda, beautiful dancer inside and out
—L. N.

To Tom, a prince among felines
—C. A.-E.

Artist's Note

For the paintings, I first sketched out the pages. Then, after revisions, I transferred the drawings onto 90 lb. hot-press Arches paper. I used gouache to fill in the color, and then I went over everything with layers of colored pencil to add shading and detail. Hopefully, together Ms. Newman and I have created a character who will appeal to aspiring ballerinas and, um, "ballerdudes" everywhere!

Cataloging-in-Publication Data has been applied for and may be obtained from the Library of Congress.
ISBN 978-0-8109-8396-0

Text copyright © 2010 Lesléa Newman
Illustrations copyright © 2010 Carey Armstrong-Ellis
Book design by Maria T. Middleton

Printed and bound in China
10 9 8 7 6 5 4 3 2 1

ABRAMS
THE ART OF BOOKS SINCE 1949

115 West 18th Street
New York, NY 10011
www.abramsbooks.com